Tofylis, or The Marriage of Zosė

Tofylis, or The Marriage of Zosė
Žemaitė
Translated from the Lithuanian by Violeta Kelertas

PAPER
+ INK

Tofylis, or The Marriage of Zosė by Žemaitė

This edition has been published in 2018
in the United Kingdom by Paper + Ink.

www.paperand.ink
Twitter: @paper_andink
Instagram: paper_and.ink

"Tofylis" was first published in 1897 in *Vienybė lietuvininkų*
magazine (Plymouth, Pennsylvania, USA).

English translation © Violeta Kelertas, 2018
This translation was originally undertaken under the auspices of
the Bernice Kellogg Endowment at the University of Washington, Seattle.

1 2 3 4 5 6 7 8 9 10

ISBN 9781911475347

This book has been published with support from
the Lithuanian Culture Institute.

A CIP catalogue record for this book is available from the British Library.

Jacket design by James Nunn: www.jamesnunn.co.uk | @Gnunkse

Printed and bound in Poland by Opolgraf: www.opolgraf.com

TRANSLATOR'S NOTE

"Tofylis" was first published in 1897 in *Vienybė lietuvininkų*, a weekly Lithuanian newspaper in the United States; a Tsarist press ban in Lithuania prohibited publications using alphabets other than Cyrillic. Forbidden books were published in either East Prussia or the US, and imported by smugglers. (The ban is also the reason Julija Beniuševičiūtė-Žymantienė used a pseudonym, choosing "Žemaitė".)

TOFYLIS, OR THE MARRIAGE OF ZOSĖ

Rain and more rain, the whole day through! It was as if the bright, sunny weather was never going to come again. Everywhere you looked, there was a misty, overcast sky. The wind came from the west and the clouds scudded and scurried to the east, billowing the rain in fine drops that were nevertheless so abundant that the ground overflowed with water. On the sand, a person's foot sank in very deep – that's how soaked the grass was already –

while in the hollows of the hard-packed gravel, as far as the eye could see, lay countless, bubbling puddles. In the low spots, pure water rippled.

In such foul weather, even the little birds didn't fly through the air – puffed up, they hid somewhere under wet leaves. At home, the hens cowered under the eaves; only out of great necessity, at the rooster's urging, did they wade to the worms with their feathers tucked under. The pigeons that had crept into the roof's ridge cooed, scuffled and kissed. The ducks seemed to be having a good time! Quacking and muddy, they waddled, hurrying from one puddle to the next, and plunged into every one, right up to their eyes. The working people couldn't labour in the fields; they all picked at something tedious under shelter. It was only here and there that one could see the men, their trousers rolled up, wading with chains and bridles in their hands. And those miserable little shepherd boys! For them, there's no such thing as bad weather; all wet, through and through, they slid about, around their little herds.

Toward evening, the light wind quieted down a bit, the rain dwindled and the clouds slipped away to the east; in the west, at the edge of the clouds, the red, setting sun took a good, long look. On the opposite side, at the other edge of the sky, the clear corner of a rainbow appeared; for a short time all the roadsides lit up, but soon the sun fell behind the woods and the rainbow died away. Here and there, a small star flickered in the gaps among the clouds. The shepherd boy played his pipe; the herd rattled and clattered toward home. Water dripped from the leaves of the drooping tree branches in the orchard; as the wind gusted, the trees stirred, and the drops scattered on the sandy paths.

At the end of the orchard, to the north, there were two dense rows of spruce trees. The road between them had been raked and strewn with sand, and was a bit sodden from the day's rain; at the end of the lane, in the dense shrubbery, was a small bench; in front of it, a round rock had been placed on a post. Sitting on that bench in the thicket, a young girl sobbed bitterly.

The moon had risen; passing through the clouds, it watched through the gaps in the branches, as if wishing to ask: *Little one, why are you crying?* The wind puffed straight into the girl's face and tousled her golden hair, as if it wanted to cool off her red cheeks, all hot from the tears rolling down them. Her breast rose and fell with pain, and her sighs were deep. She clasped her hands and lowered them onto her lap, fixing her light-blue eyes – red with weeping – far, far away on the dawn's glow; but she didn't even see the stars there. In the depths of her mind stood the vivid picture of a man of graceful build, curly-haired and blue-eyed, with a brownish moustache and beard. The girl thought of him ardently:

"How many nights have I waited here till late! And he's nowhere in sight ... At first, *he* would always be the one waiting for *me*, or as soon as I got here at a run, I'd feel him jumping over the rail fence. Embracing me, he'd press me passionately to his heart ... or, kneeling in front of me, he'd kiss the fingers of my hand, one by

11

one ... And the affection in his words! I'll never forget how he said, 'Zosė, darling, you're my sweetheart! You're more beautiful than all the beauteous things in the world, you're more precious to me than all precious things, more sweet to my heart than all sweet things, to my eyes you're brighter than all the stars in the sky! ... I can't live without you, I couldn't make it through one day without seeing you! ... You're the joy of my heart! Words can't say how much I love you, and shall love you forever!

"'If I'm lying,' he said, 'may thunder strike me this minute, or may the earth open up and swallow me! May I fall into Hell alive!' He crossed himself, called on the name of the Lord God, kissed my rosary! Why, who would doubt such oaths? Who could even imagine that they could be lies!"

The branches whispered. Zosė stirred as if awakened from sleep, and looked around: no one was there. Tears streamed down her face again, and she let out a sigh.

"Dear God! What am I going to do, if he leaves me and won't marry me! He won't even come near me; I can't even tell him that I wait for him here every night. Before, we'd understand each other from one glance, one blink ... and now he doesn't even understand my words! Maybe he's angry about something? Maybe I did something that put him off? But why should he cause me such misery, cause my heart such woe? Couldn't he just tell me straight out if he doesn't like something? Don't I listen to him? He forbade me to dance, to go to gatherings ... He won't allow me to sing ... and now he won't let me talk to anybody ... I obey all of it,

I've listened to every one of his orders ... Because of that, everyone started making fun of me, pointing fingers at me. But I wouldn't care about anything, if he just loved me ... Oh, wretched me! I see a great change in his love."

The girl's tears were now the size of beans.

"It's true ... my mistress and the house-keeper warned me not to trust any young man. There were several who had bothered me. Even the master himself did – catching me off guard somewhere, he didn't just kiss me on the mouth and hands – but I got rid of them all successfully, because not one of them touched my heart so deeply! But Tofylis, even though he doesn't suit any of the girls – all of them speak ill of him, and I can hear and see for myself that he swears and he's stubborn, but that doesn't matter at all. He has enslaved me; let the whole world shout that he won't be kind to his wife, I won't be afraid. If only he makes me his, I'll do all in my power to bend him to me, to nurse him, obey him and love him without end ... And he'll love me too then, even if I have to suffer in poverty, even if I lose everything and go hungry, I'll manage to bear everything just so I get to love him!

"To *love*," thought the girl. "Who can forbid me to love him? Even if he deserts me, I can love him in my heart ... but what shall I do if he leaves me? How many times has Mother told me, 'Be careful, my child! If you get in the family way, don't even show your face around me – I'll renounce you forever!' She won't take me in, she won't feel sorry for me, I can't even complain to her! I'd rush to the mistress, but she'll let me go. They'll drive me out on the spot! She'll say, 'Why didn't you listen to me!' Where shall I go, then? I won't be able to do anything. I won't find protection anywhere ... unless death takes pity on me; let it come quickly!"

An owl hooted right over the girl's head. She jumped up, terribly frightened, and ran home without a backward glance.

A round table stood at the centre of the warm, perfumed room papered in gilt fabric, on a shiny floor surrounded by soft rocking chairs. A lamp as bright as the sun was suspended from the ceiling on sparkling chains, just above the middle of the table. Half the table surface was covered with scattered sheaves of newspapers. Seated at one end, the master was reading a section. His hair was standing on end, dark and shiny as if it had been tarred. His eyes were as big as June beetles; it seemed as though he skewered whatever he looked at. He was a young man with rosy cheeks, curled whiskers, a cheerful face and a handsome figure.

The lady was dazzling, too, with a complexion of cherries and snow, blue eyes and curly yellow bangs fluffed up on her forehead. A row of sparkling little gemstones, knotted in gold, shone under her neck; her fitted, ornamented clothes constricted her waist; a tiny watch attached to a gold chain hung on her chest, and gold bracelets ornamented her wrists. Her face, although heavily dusted with white powder, revealed her to be older than the master by a fair bit. Two small *demoiselles*, dressed up like dolls, amused themselves by rolling gold rings across the table; glancing at her watch, a nanny, no longer young, watched them; the little one started to whimper for some reason, and the lady said to the nanny:

"It's already time for the little misses to be off to bed! Take them to the bedroom, light the green lantern and call Zosė – let her make up their beds."

"I wonder how I'm supposed to call that girl," muttered the nanny to herself. "She was in tears, snivelling all afternoon, then in the evening, she disappeared somewhere. Probably she fell asleep, hidden away someplace ... Easy for her, while I don't have a moment's rest! I have to stay as if I'm attached or bound to them." The nanny went off grumbling, carrying one child and leading the other.

The lady gathered up her rings and put them on her fingers. Seating herself, she said: "There's nothing but trouble with these maids! It's the same with Zosė: before, it seemed there weren't words to describe her diligence, and now suddenly she's become impossible. Tell her to do one thing, and when you look she's doing something else entirely; call her to get you something, and when you look, she's handing you something else ... She's all mixed up! It's like she's gone mad, like she's fallen in love ... Probably someone has turned her head, or utterly deceived her. That accursed way of men, married or not – they stick to the young girls like tar to a wheel, and spoil them completely."

While saying this, she paid attention to the impression her speech was making on the master. Continuing his reading, he had already started smiling. Throwing down his paper and nodding his head, he laughed.

"You silly fool, you," he said to his wife, "I knew what you were going to say the moment you opened your mouth. Comparing me to that kind of trash! If I had a mind to it, wouldn't I find someone more worth my while? But I'm not that kind of man; I don't need it. There could be girls by the hundreds, even the most beautiful, rolling around at my feet – not a one would stick to me, nor lead me astray. Isn't it allowed, as a joke, to praise some pretty girl? But to tell the truth, if one did start hanging around me, I'd give her such a cuff on the cheek, she'd have to lick herself off, no less!"

Laughing, the master and mistress kissed. They pulled the bell. At the sound a servant, a tall, decent fellow, ran in and asked: "Your wish, Madam?"

"I was calling Zosė, not you!" said the mistress.

"She's not here; the nanny called for her, and looked for her – she couldn't find her anywhere." The servant finished with a laugh. "Probably she ran off with Tofylis!"

The master fixed his eyes on the servant. Amazed, the mistress asked: "What? Zosė running to Tofylis?! What's this you're going on about?"

"It's true, Madam! The maid fell in love – she's hopelessly stuck on the fellow. She's running after him, shouting and wailing; he can't get rid of her anymore."

Shaking her head, the mistress lit a candle and carried it out the door.

"You can go to bed!" the master said to the servant. He himself went out. Making his way down the hall, he knocked at one door.

"I'm here!" was the reply from inside.

"Bring me some cold water."

Having given his order, the master went into a different room. Hard on his heels, Zosė brought in a glass of water. Setting it down on a little table, she tried to hurry away, but the master grabbed her into his embrace. He spoke quietly and quickly: "So, you little liar! You said, *'I've never loved anyone, and never will!'* I see you can love Tofylis, though; while me, you can't! Give me a kiss, at least!"

Turning, Zosė suddenly pushed the master in the chest, causing him to lose his balance. "Get away!" she cried. "You are not my social equal, so don't bother me. I've told you many times, and if you don't listen, I'll tell the lady right away."

"Hush, you fool!" the master bade her

as she rushed out the door. "Be quiet!"
Lighting a candle, he went to look in on
his children, and whispered something
quietly to the nanny. She didn't reply,
merely nodded her head: *all right, all
right*.

Sitting in front of a huge mirror, the
mistress was twisting her hair on little
papers while Zosė made up the bed. The
lady was the first to speak:

"I never expected that you would
be so wanton, as I see now. Aren't you
ashamed to go running after the young
men yourself? It's fortunate the master
doesn't have anything to do with you, but
if, just for a joke, he were to tease you, he

wouldn't be able to get rid of you after that! You shameless hussies! Just you run out in the evening again, I'll immediately let you go or tell your mother! You'll get to hear things you've never heard before – or she'll give you a whipping. The young men won't stick up for you then. She asks me to watch you, but you don't obey me. It's her business, let her watch you herself! What are you thinking? Are you looking for trouble? That fellow will soon make a fool of you, especially one like Tofylis – he's sharp, been around; he's decent. He's not your equal, nor will he take you to wife! And where will you go after that? Who's going to take you in? Whomever you blame will just scorn you, poke fun at you … and what will you do to him? Everyone will blame you; you won't find anyone to protect you. No one will comfort you, because, to tell the truth, the girls are always more to blame than the fellows."

The mistress went on and on, repeating the same thing over and over, even though Zosė was long gone. Having done her chores and closed herself up in her little room, she prostrated herself on the floor before the crucifix there, arms outstretched. Breathless from weeping, she cried: "Oh God, most merciful! Take pity on me, accept me into the black earth, take me from this life, cover me from people's eyes, save me from evil tongues ... take my life this very night ...!"

In the stable, in the coachmen's room, the manor serfs had gathered and were playing cards. They played for money or drinks; when those were gone, they played for matches. Bored, they left off playing, and joked around.

"Enough, that's enough of cards," said the huntsman. "It would all be very well to play with those who pay, but not a one of you does! Well, when I was by Prince Bibikov, we'd get together for cards, we'd heat up the samovar, you'd have your fill of sugar and rum, we'd make merry, raise a ruckus the whole night through. The dames would come in, too – matchmakers' wives, chambermaids, all dolled up, my respect to them. Did they ever cling to me like flies to honey! One says, 'Pan Teofyl', another – 'Pan Teofyl!'"

One of the young men mimicked under his breath: "One says '*Pantofel*', another says – '*Pantofel*'!"[1]

"You fool, do you think I looked like you – you idiot?! Now I've grown slovenly, but in those days I was pomaded, perfumed, clad in britches and boots – I was a real gentleman ..."

"Yeah, yeah," the same young man laughed. "'Master Britchit!' 'Master Britchit!'"

"Shut up, you bastard!" shouted the huntsman. "Son of a bitch!" Then he continued, more quietly: "Not only the maids, but even the ladies themselves were fairly drooling when I was in service to Count Suvorov. The husband was an

---

[1] "Pan Teofyl" translates as "Mister Teofyl" (Tofylis) in Polish; the young man mocks Tofylis by playing on the name with the word *pantofel* ("slipper", also Polish), with its connotations of flimsiness and submissiveness (especially as a henpecked husband).

old man, but his wife was young; she had most certainly made up her mind to take me across the border. She said: 'You fool, don't be afraid, I'll make you happy!'

"Afterward, I was hired by the Baron von de Fleury; we went to Nizhny Novgorod, from there to Paris. One lady, a merchant's widow, had taken it into her head to marry me ... she was rich, a millionairess, yet! If she'd been a Catholic, I would have married her for sure. How much of her tobacco I smoked! I'd take it from the shop. I'd want to pay ... 'No need, no need to,' she'd shout from far off. Of course, you must have some sense, you'd have to pay her back, and I would often treat her. There was money; there was the wherewithal to drink, too.

"At a ball at Count Naikin's, he arranged a royal hunt ... The Tsar sat on his chair in the woods, and the Tsar's court and the senators drove the wild animals to him. As soon as some animal sticks its head out, immediately a footman set there for that purpose goes *whoosh!* and hands the Tsar a ready-loaded rifle. The latter goes *bang!* and shoots the animal. He just missed shooting the Governor of Vilnius. He beat a fox toward the Tsar, and squatted down himself to see him shoot. The Tsar just went *bang!* the fox's tail goes flying away, so the pellets all stuck in the Governor; afterward, they had a job getting all the pellets out ...

"They assigned us six servants at the dinner table. We dressed up in uniforms, black tailcoats, white trousers down to our knees, red stockings tied with blue ties and bows below the knees, Parisian shoes – yellow, matching – and a hat under the arm for good style. All the boys were dressed up, and I was the best-looking of all. The Minister of the Interior looked us over; he searched us so strictly that you couldn't get away with a knife or even a needle on you. He sent us to the old, bearded Orthodox priest to swear to it: in those days, for three days of service we received five roubles each as payment from the Tsar. What could you do, at least it was earnings. And the Tsar himself didn't have that money on him either, he had to borrow it from the Governor.

"Tapping me on the shoulder, the Tsar said to me in Russian: 'You're really a Lowlander?'

"'Yes, a Lowlander, but I'm a landowner,' I replied.

"'I see, I see. You're a handsome fellow. Have you been to Kražiai?'

"'Yes, I have.'

"Well, as I started to tell him how things were there, what went on, the Tsar just keeps shrugging his shoulders and looking at the Governor of Kaunas. That one kept bowing and bowing at me to prevent me from telling the whole truth … There was a time when I used to mingle with such distinguished figures, but now it's as if I've crawled into a cave here with all of you – even the money's gone, and I've become wholly common myself; even the city ladies wouldn't recognise me."

"Now even one Zosė is enough!" said the old coachman, already dozing off.

"As people say: a starving dog eats even June bugs – that's how Zosė is for me. As there is no one more respectable, no one better, she'll have to do until I get sick of her. After that, kick her aside, and that's it! I've already gone through so many like her, not for Zosė to compare herself to. But I have such splendid luck with the women! The minute the thought of one crosses my mind, I can say ahead of time that she's already mine."

"Luck ... Luck!" repeated the coachman. "To you, it may seem like luck, but for that girl, it's eternal misery."

"She got what she wanted," Tofylis retorted.

"Well, she didn't force her love on you; you, sir, must have done something to talk her into it."

"Yep, my tongue is just made for tricks! When I start to spill the compliments with skill and cheer, when I try to be pleasant, I've seduced more obstinate and prudent ones many times! As for Zosė, she's an easy one for me! I just beckoned with one finger and she stuck to me."

"That's why you can't kick such an innocent child aside, if it was the way you're boasting, that you secured her heart with your clever tongue; you shouldn't have deceived her, because you, sir, you already have a head on your shoulders, and you're not her age anymore. It's not a joke to be the undoing of a young child for the rest of her life; you have to take your own conscience into account, too."

Tofylis burst out laughing. "Ha! Scruples ... conscience ... for a maid, yet! What do I care? Let her carry on like a cat in heat! Didn't I see it! Zosė, too, would come to the evening dance, so she'd dance and sing, fool around with those scapegraces; I'd become furious. I decided: *Zosė was mine!* In a second, I pushed all those good-for-nothings away ... See, now that's

the joke – 'none for you and none for me'!"
He cackled away. "She'll know, poor soul,
that I'm not of her station."

The young man who earlier had
mimicked Teofylis's bragging now spit in
his palm and pushed his cap further back
on his head, all red in the face like a rooster.
His eyes flashed. He went over and stood
in front of Tofylis, clenching his fists. He
opened and closed his mouth, but didn't
say a word. It seemed as if his tongue
had frozen. Everyone started laughing.
He rushed out the door, and outside he
swore he was done. He started to feed the
horses, and kept wiping his tears with his
sleeve.

There were only two left in the cottage
now: Tofylis and the coachman. The latter
started in again:

"You know, Mister Tofylis, that you can't

very well compare yourself to Zosė! She's just trouble now, until she can appease her mother, and as for everything else, there's no rush. A husband will show up for her, though not right away – she's still young. She has several hundred roubles from her father's inheritance; she's young and beautiful, and besides, she knows how to sew nicely ... A wise husband won't blame her or reject her, as long as there's the money. There's just no one to take it on now, but you could get into deep trouble for your deception."

"Well, that's something new! A maid is going to do something to me! How many times does it happen, that a maid with child comes to a wedding just as the young man is marrying another. And what does she get? The parish priest shuts her into the pigpen until he finishes the ceremony;

the slut's left holding the bag!"

"It's a different case with the parish priest!" said the coachman. "If only someone would wise up the mother, hand a hundred or so to the lawyer, so they could catch hold of the gentleman by his fur coat! In this case, it's very simple: it's a good judgement. The lass is maybe seventeen, and the lover is more than twice her age. So the court would just shear the ram. It's up to you, but in reality, look to marriage. The mother wouldn't even want her to marry you; she hopes to give her to someone who works his own land."

Giving this a bit of thought, Tofylis asked: "Where does the mother keep this money? Probably she gets interest, or has put it in a bank somewhere?"

"How's she going to give it up for interest, a cunning old woman like that!

Probably she keeps it next to her, hides it, doesn't boast to anyone that she has it ... In the end, even Zosė doesn't know about it; just my wife knows, as she's her relative ... She showed her maybe five hundred, saying, 'Father left this for little Zosė; when she gets married, I'll give it to her.'"

Tofylis was silent. The coachman, lighting his pipe, spoke again: "I don't understand the young men of this era, and their 'love' ... All they look for is just to sneak up on someone, just to deceive her! It doesn't matter what kind of girl it is, from what class ... And they boast of it, even take pride in it. Bah, what kind of love is that? The Devil take it! In other times – before I chose my wife – it used to be, if I liked some girl, I'd watch her from afar, I'd look her over this way and that way, I'd ask her questions ... but

I wouldn't show her that I liked her. If I just noticed some flaw on her, to the Devil with her! Without any embarrassment, or any fault-finding. And when I met my own, how I fell in love with her; not even a hundred devils could have distracted me. I was ready to jump into water or fire, if I could just win her heart. But first to love and tempt a girl, then when you're bored, to ridicule her and kick her away – only a hopeless rogue can do that!"

Clearing his throat, Tofylis said: "Mister Katauskis! You are a friendly man, and you've tasted bread from many an oven; you have so much wisdom, and you understand that I am in a position to catch someone worthier than Zosė ... but I'm not that kind of person; even though she's a very beggarly girl, I won't leave her. As people say, you only go blind once.

After getting married, I'll only have death to worry about. Goodnight, for now! Next time, we'll talk more."

When he went inside to bed, the coachman related his chat with Tofylis, laughing.

The small, decrepit, old cottage looked shabby from the exterior, but inside it was very clean. The dirt floor had been swept with a broom and scattered with sand; the windows and table had been polished, the bed made up in white. A woman, no longer young, with a scarf tied around her head, was working at something under the window –she was probably the housewife of the little cottage. A second one, younger by a good measure, finely dressed, hopped in through the doorway.

"May Jesus Christ be honoured! Auntie, what are you doing?"

"It's been a long time! Forever and ever! What brings you here? All the manor dogs must have hanged themselves, if you've showed up. I was just meaning to go by you, to see if you've all croaked or what. Even Zosė never passes by. What's new at the manor? Have a seat."

"Oh, what can be new there, Auntie? We just run hither and yon, and stir around like peas in a soup."

"And I do as well," said the old woman, sitting down. "I dream every night. I'm exhausted and done for, I'm wading through mud, and always around the manor. I keep getting ready to go see Zosė, but it seems I don't dare to hang around there. I'll wait every day; maybe she'll get away, the scamp. She doesn't even miss me!"

"Auntie, it's the work, you know ... you can't just fly off whenever you get it into your head." The woman strained her words through clenched teeth, looking her aunt straight in the eye. "Something's up with Zosė, too ... she's become so unhappy. She has no joy left in her; she doesn't go anywhere ... she rarely runs over to see us, either."

"Maybe the mistress prevents her?" asked the old one.

"I wonder, Auntie, if it's the mistress who tires her out, or if she can't handle the work. She's so pale ... often, she looks like she's drowning in tears ... maybe she's sick, or the food doesn't agree with her. I don't know what to think ... but Zosė's changed a great deal!"

"Stop your whimpering," the old one said angrily. "Could it be that the Devil has already made a mockery of Zosė? Well, if the Devil led her astray and it's turned out badly" – she pounded the table with her fist – "then the child will find out what Jesus's grace is!"

"Auntie dear, your child is still your child! Even if it was that way, you couldn't do anything about it; you'd have to forgive her."

"I couldn't do anything ... what are you going on about now?" shouted the old woman, turning as red as a hen turkey. "Forgive? What kind of talk is that? *Couldn't do anything?* I'd beat her – I'd beat that good-for-nothing with all my might! I'd thrash you and your husband and that lover of hers, wherever the blows happened to land ... I'd poke the master's and mistress's eyes out!" The old woman wailed on, running out of breath.

Pacing the dirt floor, she grabbed one thing, threw another and seized something else again: first a washrag, then a cup. She pushed a chair forward and then pulled it back; she ran riot, raged and cursed Zosė, sent her to the Devil.

The younger woman laughed to herself, watching this fury; afterward, she said: "And what would you do, Auntie ...? You'd whip all of them in turn, and in the end you'd get tired and forgive her!"

"You're going to wait in vain for that! But just wait, you loathsome creature," she threatened, coming closer. "You're raising children, too – you don't know what can happen to your girls!"

"Of course, Auntie, I'm raising them and loving them, but I don't know how they'll turn out; I only know this for sure: as long as I'm alive, in my child's greatest misfortune or sin, I'll never renounce them. I'll always help and give them shelter the best I know how."

"If you stick up for profligates, probably you were the same way yourself. But I wasn't! Look at us, we were five sisters; some of us weren't all that young when we married, but did any one of us turn wanton? Among our kinsfolk, there wasn't a single wench with child, and there won't be! I renounce Zosė, if that's what's happened! I don't want to lay eyes on her! May she drop dead this minute, and her bastard, too! I'll damn him, I'll kill him!"

"Stop, Auntie, don't curse without cause. After all, you haven't seen anything yet, any debauchery. Tofylis, the head of our hunters, fell in love, and is stuck on marrying Zosė. He's asking my man to be the matchmaker. That's why the child's sad and full of cares, but there's nothing bad to be seen between them. Every girl getting married worries."

"That's what you should say, then," said the old woman, settling down a little.

"It's just that we don't much care for that beau of hers, Auntie. We can't figure out whether to help the match or to hinder it ... we're worried the girl will be ruined for life. Maybe it would be better for her to live in poverty alone, even if, God forbid, she's left with a child?"

"What kind of talk is that! 'Don't care for' ... 'So she wouldn't be ruined'... a married woman is never ruined! A husband is worth a bit more than a devil, as long as he's not a cripple and can feed his wife. I won't put an end to it. I won't tarry, don't expect it. As long as he takes Zosė to wife, I'll try to please him and give everything I can think of to my dear son-in-law ... Let your husband make the match. Let's not wait till the trouble begins. Don't even think of it then – they won't get anything out of me. I'd renounce Zosė for all time!"

The autumn days were sunny and bright, but the wind was biting. The noses of the women doing the washing by the pond had turned as red as plums, but without paying attention to the cold and to the north wind, they did their work cheerfully, joking around. And when they burst out singing, how the fields resounded! Zosė sang first, and the others took up the singing; the heartier the song, the more quickly the women busied themselves with the laundry. Zosė hurried at a run, helping them all; she glanced around, grabbed a pile of clothing, ran off, hung everything up and returned again, singing, to busy herself.

"Take care, dear Zosė, to return the laundry white this last time," said the coachman's wife. "I think the mistress will remember your work. Will the next one be able to do as good a job at satisfying her? Wonder what kind of chambermaid they'll bring home tonight!"

"Zosė's worked for her faithfully for several years," said one of the women. "That's why the mistress will arrange a decent wedding for her."

"I'd say so!" added another. "Just look at the housekeeper: she's furious that she has to get everything ready, make beer, bake cakes."

"See, she's too lazy! You'd think she begrudges the master's riches. Why should she be reluctant, as long as the masters aren't being cheap."

"My masters are kind to me, really kind!" Zosė praised them. "Not only are they having a wedding for me, but they gave me such a gift! May God reward them! They bought me a brand-new sewing machine, which cost quite a bit. Where else are you going to find such masters?"

"Girls, do you know something?" said a rather old woman. "If I were Zosė, I wouldn't throw a second glance at that 'Toffer'! Girl, what did you see in him? He's not even an honest person! He only knows how to live by his tongue: first he harps on one, then another, telling the master all kinds of stories and informing on them. Everyone's fed up with it."

"It's always the decent girl who ends up with a bad young man. Is that 'Toffer' going to be a good husband? The child in all her youth will be ruined, she'll fall into the whey like a little fly. If I were her mother, I wouldn't let her marry him; he doesn't suit me, either."

The women talked amongst themselves under their breath. Then one of them asked Zosė: "And where is that 'Toffer' going to take you after the wedding?"

"Nowhere. We're going to stay here until Tofylis's year is up. The masters are keeping me; they don't begrudge me the bread."

"Zosė! ... Zosė!" someone was calling from behind them.

All the women turned around. Tofylis was coming their way, clutching a white bundle.

"What's all this blabbering about?" he said to Zosė. "Your ears must have been so stuffed up that you didn't hear me calling! Why didn't you collect my dirty white shirts to wash?"

"I did collect them," Zosė said. "I did look for them – I couldn't find any more."

"And you couldn't ask me! You're a real fool, no use explaining to someone like that. Because of you, I had to carry them all this way myself. Here, wash these, too."

He threw the bundle he'd brought at Zosė with such force that the shirts spread all over her head. They turned out to be hideously soiled, and Zosė cast them off. The women glanced at each other.

"Why, you scoundrel!" yelled the coachman's wife. "You're just lucky that Zosė isn't mean. If it was me, you'd part with your curls for doing something like that!"

"Forgive me, my dear lady!" Tofylis bent

down, raising his cap. "I was aiming for the legs – but instead I hit her head." He left, laughing.

The old mother spent almost the entire evening looking out the windows: no matter where she was, she'd keep rushing up to one. She'd look around the cottage, open a cupboard, look inside, wave the flies away from the cups and look out the window again.

"Probably she's spread her legs," she muttered to herself. "It's almost eventide, and she's still not here."

Raising the lid of the chest, she turned over the scarves and rummaged around; closing the chest, she went to the window again. Finally, the dog let out a bark and ran up to someone. Zosė came in, all out of breath, and kissed her mother's hand.

"Where are the other two?" asked the mother. "Why are you so late? A body's waiting in vain ..."

"They're coming right away. They stayed back a little." Zosė fell to her knees before her mother, grasped her hands, kissed them and begged her, weeping: "Mother, dear Mother! Have mercy on me, have mercy!"

"What's happened to you? What do you want? Have you lost your mind? Why are you crying – tell me!"

"Mother dear, my sweet! Help me – don't let me get married, take me in by myself. I'll work and do my best ... I'll sew ... everything I earn, I'll give to you ..."

"For the love of God! Have you taken leave of your wits?"

"No, Mother, I haven't, I've *found* my

wits! My eyes have been opened. I see that I'll be lost with him. He doesn't love me, and he's running me ragged now already. Better to stay unmarried, to suffer once than to weep all my life. All the women are telling me to ... Mama, take pity!"

"Why, you good-for-nothing, you horrible creature!" shouted the mother, jumping back. "What other nonsense will you think up! To listen to women's tongues? And you want to shove your bastard on me to raise? No, that will never be! He suited you before, he has to suit you now, too. You have to bow at his feet, even, as he hasn't left you after sullying you. Don't you dare! I don't want to hear anymore of that! And if you start with your antics again, you'll see, I'll take a stick and beat your hide! Or else get out of my sight! So I don't see you or your bastard anymore!"

Just then the coachman and Tofylis came clattering in, both of them having taken a drop; making a racket on the dirt floor, they set a flask of vodka on the table. Zosė's mother set out some food to nibble on, and called everyone in to partake.

"Mama dear, bottoms up! To the bottom, please!"

"I can't, my dear son-in-law, I can't! It's so strong!"

"If you don't drink up, it must be that you don't love me, Mama dear!"

"How can I not love such a curly-locks!" said the mother, caressing Tofylis. "How handsome my son-in-law is, like a double-leafed clover! Every one of your locks is worth a hundred roubles."

"When I was in the cities," Tofylis began to recount, puffing out his chest, "in Paris, with Count Golubov, I had no truck with –"

"What's the long speech for?" the coachman interrupted. "I have to hurry home. Get on with it ..."

"Now, then! We'll have to have a talk! Here, I'll show Mother the wedding rings I bought." Tofylis pushed the rings across the table.

"Oh my, how they shine!" The mother rejoiced, rubbing the rings between her fingers.

"That's because they're expensive," pronounced Tofylis. "They're made of real gold, *dente* ..."

"What's *dente*?" asked the mother.

"That word in Polish spells out thick or cast gold. Other rings or brooches are hollow, curved; in Polish, that's called *masiv*. That kind of gold is cheaper, while these rings of mine are more expensive. No one can cheat me, I know what things cost."

"Why did you buy such expensive ones?

Cheaper ones would have done as well."

"I'm no commoner, and no country bumpkin. If I'm buying something, even if it is the most expensive, it has to be a reliable, splendid thing; while something cheap, of poor quality, isn't worth buying. The amount of gold that has gone through my hands! When I was in the service of Mister Zulikov in Novo-Alexandrovskoye, there were shops upon shops –"

"You're losing your train of thought, Mister Teofyl!" interrupted the coachman. "You've paid your respects to Mother dear – better say briefly what you came for. Anyway, she herself has an idea as to what it is we're short of before the wedding."

"Oh, I know only too well that money is always needed, but I, too, don't have too much of it ..." Scratching her head, the mother opened the chest and took out a small folded-up paper, unwound a stack of banknotes from it and set it on the table in front of Zosė. "Here, dear child," she said to Zosė, "are your five tens. I don't know if this makes a hundred roubles. You yourself earned them, and put them away by me; take them back yourself now or give them to your husband, it's in your hands ..."

Without a moment's hesitation, Tofylis snatched the money, saying: "My dear little Zosė, my sweet, now I am your guardian. Whatever you need is in my care, while you will just respect me, obey me, carry out my orders; whether you've done something good or bad, you'll never lie to me – you'll be loved. I have a good heart: I love those who are obedient to me very much. With submissiveness, you can drag the last thing out of me. If we were having the wedding in the city, you'd see all the things we'd have: all kinds of drinks, cakes, mugs of beer, a band playing ... I'd hire coaches to take the guests around. That's the kind of person I am: if I do something, I do it finely and splendidly. That's why, wherever I appeared in the city, they always called me a magnate. Once we drove to Chernogorsk, an endlessly big city –"

"Mother, dear!" interrupted the coachman, "You gave Zosė back her own money, but aren't you going to add some yourself for their start?"

"Dear children, what kind of addition is it you want? After all, whatever I have, any little crumbs – it'll all go to you anyway: I have only the one child; she'll look after me in my old age, and she'll get it all. Dear son-in-law, I see that you are the best of men, you'll love your wife. You probably won't abandon me in my old age; in return, we'll love you endlessly."

Tofylis, having downed a great deal of vodka, found himself moved by the mother's praise, and was overcome by such magnanimity that he kissed her hands and feet sincerely, and was practically in tears as he spoke: "Oh sweet, dear Mama! I swear to God, neither you nor Zosie will ever hear a coarse word from me. Holy Angel, protect me! I'd rather dive into Hell alive than cause you any grief!"

"That's enough, enough, my darling, my heart's delight!" said the mother, crying, caressing and kissing Tofylis. "With such a dear son-in-law, at least I'll end my days happily!"

Zosė, who had been sad earlier, now wiped away a tear of joy, thanking her

Mama in her heart that she had rebuked her, and hadn't let her leave such a dear husband.

Now Zosė was cheerful, satisfied for life; in the end, she had achieved what she had so greatly desired: Tofylis's love would not end until death's door.

After the wedding, having moved into her husband's little chamber, she made her nest for life. She fixed it up and cleaned out the corners. Looking through his clothes, she found them in a sorry state; she brought back a couple of rolls of linen from her mother's, and sewed the necessary items for her husband. Nothing brought her more joy than the machine:

it ran so smoothly, like a knife through butter.

In the evening, when her husband had come home from the woods, she petted him, kissed him, warmed him up, took his shoes off, gave him the dinner she'd kept warm, made pleasant conversation. Then she showed him her day's work, saying: "Tofyl, here, I sewed you eight shirts. There'll be four more. Look, do the collars fit?"

"With that kind of shirt," said Tofylis, looking askance, "I'll have to turn into a real bumpkin. I can't remember the last time I wore homespun clothes. They're going to scratch my back like crazy."

"Dear heart, now you'll *have* to wear homespun clothes, for your shop-bought ones are all in rags; and these, never fear, they won't scratch. It's such thin linen, I'll iron them yet – they'll be like cotton."

"What kind of sewing is this? Phew," sputtered Tofylis, turning the shirts this way and that. "The sleeves are like bags, the pleats are like a skirt's, the collars like sausages. If you didn't know how to do it, you should have asked me; I would have taught you how to sew to shape. You don't know, you haven't ever seen a properly sewn shirt. You're used to the peasant style, so you want to dress me like that? You can't compare yourself to me; wear them yourself!"

Grumbling, he lit a cigarette and went to bed.

His words bounced off Zosė as though off a hard wall. After all, she had made such a proud presentation of her skills to her husband. Her forehead turned red from pain and annoyance, while her machine rotated quickly and rattled until late.

Zosė had scarcely managed to sew enough for her husband before the manor folk overwhelmed her with work: young men bought linen, percale or homespun cloth and begged and entreated her to sew for them, as Zosė was very talented. As it turned out, she couldn't keep up with her sewing; not a day went by that she didn't earn a few gold coins.

As evening fell, when they finished their work, the manor folk stopped by Zosė's; one came to pick up his work, another to hand it in, yet another to get fitted or to pay. Upon returning home, her husband always found Zosė with someone. The first time, he frowned; the next time, he muttered; finally, one evening when the fellows had left, he scolded his wife angrily:

"You slut! Remember, Zosė, you'll make me run out of patience! I'm going to whip you *and* those fellows of yours! Only I'm just not that kind of person; I didn't want to bring shame on your head tonight. But just let me find them here next time and remember, you'll give up your hide."

Frightened, her eyes huge, Zosė looked at her husband without understanding the cause of his vexation; afterward, kissing him on his hand, she asked pleasantly: "Tofylis, my sweet! Why are you so upset? What did you see that was so bad here? Why, the kids come to pick up their sewn items – is that why you're angry, that I made three roubles for your tobacco this week?" Saying this, she reached over to kiss her husband on the lips.

"Get the hell off!" Tofylis shoved Zosė away: "I don't ask for your earnings – you get your bread on my back, so feed on it! If I see you sewing again, I'll chop up the machine with my axe, and the same will happen to you! I'm telling you straight: don't you dare sew for those hooligans, if you want to wear your hide in health."

What was there to be done? Zosė had to obey her wise husband. She finished her work for one customer, and for another she didn't; but she gave everyone their sewing and told them she had broken her needle and couldn't sew anymore. Then she put the machine away in the chest.

Without any work, Zosė grew bored; she brought a few dozen skeins of flax home from her mother's and borrowed a spinning wheel. When Tofylis came home in the evening, he found Zosė spinning. Jumping up, she took her husband's coat off, kissed him all over, caressed him, gave

him something to eat, made up his bed
and then sat down to spin. The spinning
wheel rattled a bit.

"Well, if there's one thing I can't stand,
it's that accursed spinning!" said Tofylis as
he ate. "Even my ears hurt from that racket.
To the Devil with that goat – otherwise,
I'll kick it so it'll shatter into a thousand
pieces! What a devil of a worker! She'll
take up spinning to show off her diligence
or to make me mad. You have to work at
the things that I can't bear!"

Silently, Zosė put the spinning wheel in
the corner and asked, laughing: "So what
am I going to work at now?"

"Stick your finger up your arse and
dance a sweet dance! So she's still going
to tease me like a shepherd boy! I didn't
herd pigs with you, you drudge! Lout!
That's all the understanding you have: you

don't know how lucky you are to have me!
Anyone else in my shoes wouldn't have
done a favour like that for you. You'd have
been hugging a dog around its neck and
bawling by now."

Muttering like that, he put on his cap
and went out somewhere.

Giving way to sadness, Zosė pondered
and pondered, and waited for her husband
until late; but she didn't notice when he
finally came home to bed.

For Zosė, a whole day without any work
would drag out terribly. She roamed here
and there. Afterward, when she went by
the lady's, she asked for something to
read. The mistress, knowing how much
Zosė liked to read, loaded up a whole pile
of books for her. Joyfully, Zosė brought
home an armful.

In the evening, her husband came

home to find Zosė with a book in her hand. Quickly throwing the book down on the table, she danced attendance and rushed around her dear husband, fixing up or handing him whatever he desired. You would think he'd have no cause to be angry; on the contrary, this evening he was in such a good mood that he even related a few events he'd experienced once upon a time in town. After he got tired of an audience of one, he went out to the coachman's for cards.

Zosė picked up her book again. After an hour, the husband came home to go to bed. As soon as he came through the door, he let loose at his wife like a madman: "Devil worshiper! Have you made a covenant with the Devil? To sit the whole night through, absorbed in the library! Here's where your book belongs!"

Saying this, he grabbed the book from his wife's hands and threw it under the bed. "You wastrel! To keep the lantern burning for such nonsense! You'd be better off taking up some kind of work! Only fools read – and they get in a frenzy, they go mad, while you? Even without those books, you don't have much in your head ... by reading you'll lose what little you have." Reviling all readers in general, he extinguished the light and lay down.

Pain gripped at Zosė's heart as though with pliers; she even broke out in a sweat. For a long, long time she remained kneeling, cupping her face in her hands before the picture of the Crucifixion, praying fiercely to have patience.

In the daytime, after her husband had left, Zosė lost herself in a book again; she was sat at the table with her back to the door when she felt a man's arm embracing her head; then someone kissed her. A sweet warmth overtook Zosė's heart from joy that her husband was greeting her so unexpectedly, and so affectionately. She pressed her back to his chest lovingly and cast a glance.

It was the master!

Zosė jumped up as if she'd been burned; she stood in front of him, blushing, and pierced him with her eyes as if asking him: *Why are you here?*, because in her fear and infuriation she could not utter a word. The master, smiling pleasantly, held out his hand to her, saying:

"Zosė, dear, won't you come to your senses? You can see that I love you, and have done you so much good! Now you can love me boldly, without fear – because under cover of your husband, you won't surround yourself with gossip, and you'll have a lot to gain from me." He took her by the hand. "Agreed?"

Retreating a few steps, Zosė retorted in a trembling voice: "No, no! I don't even want to see you, sir!"

In the evening, Tofylis came home in a very good mood. He was cheerful, and talked a lot, but reeked of spirits.

As was her habit, Zosė removed her husband's coat and served him in silence. She was sad for some reason, and walked around, distressed. Her husband caught wind of this; embracing his wife, pulling her onto his lap and fondling her, he asked:

"Dear soul, why are you so unhappy? You look like you're scared of something. Is there something you need? Ask without fear, tell me, I'm the one who stands up for you and protects you. If anyone should insult you with so much as a hurtful word, you know I'm prepared to jump into fire or water for you."

Taking courage from her husband's tenderness, she related that day's incident with the master. Tofylis, showing the whites of his eyes, suddenly pushed his wife away and slapped her first across one side of the face, then the other. Zosė landed on the floor. Kicking her with his foot, his voice shaking in anger, he screamed: "Slut! Louse! Wretch! Get out, out of my sight! I told you – stay away from other men, don't be a whore!" He spat in his fury. "Now you're going to get a feel for my hand! You need convincing – you'll have to stop, for once!"

Zosė, fearing an unfortunate death from her husband's blows, falling and kneeling, was scarcely able to escape out the door and out of his sight. She would have kept running somewhere, to hide in some secret place, but she had no more strength; she could go no further ... She fell down by a fence right there, a few steps away. Everything turned dark; her ears rang, her head roared and felt shattered with pain, her heart beat with fear, her hands and legs trembled. She lay still, as though she had fainted. She couldn't sense where she was lying, or what time it was. She only heard a voice nearby asking some passing night owl: "Did you see where my wife went?"

She didn't catch the answer.

Zosė tried to sit up; overwhelmed by pain, she moaned sorrowfully. At this sound, Tofylis rushed over. Seizing his wife, who was groaning painfully, he lifted her up and rushed her inside. Shaking from the cold, Zosė threw off her outerwear. Moaning in torment, she lay down on the bed. Tofylis lit a cigarette.

"Phew! The hell with it! The steps I have to take because of your foolishness!" he griped, sitting down. "How much sleep I've lost. I had to run around everywhere. She's not by the coachman's, nor by the housekeeper's! She has to be hiding by the wayside like a partridge! Good thing it was dark, at least ... maybe nobody saw. Such fools like you slander themselves on purpose. Afterward, they'll blame the husband. I didn't even hit you! ... And she'll go running around for no good reason. Just you try it again!"

Zosė, still stunned and not yet recovered from the fear and cold, lay curled up, murmuring. She didn't catch her husband's first words, but *just you try it again!* pierced her heart terribly. She smiled bitterly at the happiness of her marriage. She envisioned its end, in the distance ... in her coffin.

Violeta Kelertas is a professor of Lithuanian Studies researching feminism, narrative theory and postcolonialism. She translates from Lithuanian into English, and is best known for her anthology of Soviet Lithuanian short stories, *Come into My Time: Lithuania in Prose Fiction, 1970–90*. Her forthcoming book contains Žemaitė's major prose works, including the writer's highly compelling autobiography.

New titles from Paper + Ink

O. Henry
The Gift of the Magi & Other Stories

Guy de Maupassant
The Necklace & Other Stories

Oscar Wilde
The Happy Prince & Other Stories

D. H. Lawrence
The Rocking Horse Winner & Other Stories

Mark Twain
*The Celebrated Jumping Frog of Calaveras County
& Other Stories*

Rūdolfs Blaumanis
In the Shadow of Death
Translated from the Latvian by Uldis Balodis

Mehis Heinsaar
The Butterfly Man & Other Stories
Translated from the Estonian by Adam Cullen and Tiina Randviir

Visit **www.paperand.ink** to subscribe and receive the other books by post, as well as to keep up to date about new volumes in the series.